For Emma

CONSTABULARY TALES

ANNE WEBER

Warmly

Anne Weber

* * * * *

* * * * *

IBSN-13: 978-1548165680

A DeWitt Studio Publication

Printed in the U.S.A

10 9 8 7 6 5 4 3 2

CONSTABULARY TALES

"Nights and days came and passed

And summer and winter and the rain

And it was good to be a little island.

A part of the world

And a world of its own

All surrounded by the bright blue sea."

Margaret Wise Brown,
The Little Island

CONTENTS

BEGINNINGS

"I think I could live here," I said to myself in the summer of 1995, here being a small island in Casco Bay, Maine. Without giving island living much more thought, I finished art school in New York City that fall, left the small upstate New York community where I raised my family and moved to the island in December. I had a head full of ideas and a heart full of sadness. I needed the solitude island life offered to regain my balance. I was 53 years old - one might say a late bloomer and no stranger to rural living.

However, the seventeen year-round residents of the island had only part of this information. They knew I was single, an artist and from New York City. George, a retired nursery owner, would become my friend and later told me my arrival was the topic of lively conversation.

"How long do you think this one will last?"

"I say she'll stay. She wears sensible boots."

"Sensible? She locked herself out of her house the first week she was here and no one EVER locks up anything."

"I'm with George. She preordered her heating oil. She'll stay."

"Alright, put your money where your mouth is. 5:1, gentlemen, 5:1."

When I fell on the ice in March and broke my right wrist, someone said, "You can pay up anytime. She'll be gone in three weeks."

I was not off to an auspicious beginning but I was determined. My reputation grew when the oil man discovered me in the crawl space under my house thawing frozen pipes with my hair dryer.

"Damn," said one of the bettors.

I painted canvases, walked in the woods and slowly became part of the community. Over the years, the old cottage I purchased was no longer "the Reverend's" but Fran's place.

In early 2000, I was pleasantly surprised and proud when my neighbors put my name up for an appointed position with the governing municipality on the mainland. Since the former job holder was the winner of the Ladies Skillet Toss at the Fryeburg fair, I knew I had big shoes to fill. The City Council approved my nomination and I agreed to become the liaison for the Police Department on the mainland with the community on the island. I was to be the new Constable, Constable Fran McNulty.

"What could go wrong?" I asked myself.

THE KAYAK RUSTLERS

On August 6, at 2:30 in the morning, I received a phone call from the mainland police station. A cottage owner had just reported someone trying to steal two kayaks from their dock on the east point of the island.

"Fran, take a ride down there and check it out," the desk sergeant said. "Call us back."

Ha, I thought as I hung up the phone. I couldn't get a vehicle down to that cottage on the cliffs even if I had one. What I did have was a bicycle. I usually put on my bike helmet with my LL Bean head lamp when I went on a night cal. When I looked out the window to check the weather I could see stars high in the sky. However, there was a thick ground fog and I knew I would be on foot.

I called the homeowner and learned that approximately 20 minutes earlier they awoke to noises down by their dock. When they turned on the porch light, they saw two people wearing hoodies trying to untie their boats. The owners yelled and both suspects ran into the woods with one of the yellow kayak paddles. They couldn't give a better description than that, except both suspects were barefoot.

I did not go on night calls alone. I had island support should I require back-up, but this week I also had house guests. I woke my friends and explained the situation. While I waited for them to get dressed, I surmised we were dealing with invaders; no island native would run through the woods at night without shoes. Nor were these local city boys because no one living close to the sea would take a boat out in this weather.

My friends appeared in the living room slightly bedraggled; one in a dress shirt, what looked like his pajama bottoms and hiking boots; the other was fully dressed in black, including thick gloves.

"I'm deputizing both of you. You are to say nothing, witness everything."

"Do we get guns?"

"No guns or weapons of any kind, guys. We are keepers of the peace, not a vigilante posse."

"You woke me up to be a sissy?"

"Listen, if things do go to hell in a hand basket," I said as I pointed to my two-way radio, "you push down this small black button and run."

"Why? What does that do?"

"It means Officer Down."

"Oh."

I grabbed the radio, three flashlights, my grumbling deputies, and headed out the door. The sounds of the fog horns didn't prepare us for what we immediately ran into. It was like swimming in the pond's murky bottom. We could not see three feet in front of us and I wondered where those thieves might end up. There were cliffs, swamps, and open well holes back in those woods--- dangerous places if you didn't know where you were going or weren't paying attention.

We made our way past the playground and halted in our tracks when we heard the old swing creaking on its chain. I turned my flashlight in that direction but the light reflected back on us and I couldn't see a thing. All our senses were heightened now as we continued to the fork leading to the scene of the crime. The old orchard on our left took on an ominous feeling as large dark shapes loomed around us and I envisioned a monster dog waiting to devour us.

When we heard eerie grunting noises somewhere ahead, the three of us gasped and froze. The hair on the back of my neck stood up. Something was out there. Was it moose, deer, rustlers? I looked at my helpers and put my finger to my lips, then pointed at some low bushes. We crouched as we hid behind them, waiting for whatever was moving in our direction. I strained my eyes and ears but the fog distorted everything. Almost immediately my back began to hurt and I knew I had to move but was afraid I would give away our position. I popped my head up quickly to get a better look. I was face-to-face with a group of figures who literally jumped out of their shoes. Our mutual screams echoed around the apple trees as everyone, including my deputies, ran in different directions. I realized I needed to identify myself.

"Stop, it's the Constable. It's Fran," I said with as much authority as I could muster. My flashlight spotted faces I recognized, a group of island teenagers and not a hoodie among them.

"You guys are out late. Where are you coming from?"

"Up…up by Kit's. We were…er… listening to music."

Music? Right. "Did you see anyone around the point? Hear anything?"

"No, Fran. We didn't hear anything."

"Well, thanks but best get yourselves home now. Some people are apparently trying to steal kayaks and it may not be safe here."

As we watched the kids disappear into the fog, I made a tactical decision. I really did not want to run into kayak rustlers in this fog. What would I do with them if I did catch them? Could I tie them to a tree until the police arrived? No, I didn't think to bring rope. Invite them back to the house for tea and biscuits? No, the biscuits were for my house guests and I wasn't in the mood to be hospitable. Besides, they weren't going anywhere till the ferries ran again in the morning. Not wanting to lose face, however, I announced to no one in particular:

"Let's head to the beach and make sure the other kayaks on the island are secure."

I was surprised when my deputies readily agreed. We headed down to the flats where the area was partially lit and a slight breeze off the water shifted the fog. We sat for a moment and gratefully realized everything here was as it should be. I breathed in the salt air and hoped my heart rate would return to normal so I could make the walk back up the hill.

I called in my report once we got home, thanked my guests for their help and went to bed.

After a few hours' sleep, I awoke and rode my bicycle down to the landing where the first boat into town was just docking. Sure enough, two scruffy young men wearing hoodies came from the path leading up to the woods. I was suspicious.

I gave them a good once-over: one approximately 5'8", dark green hoodie, black Converse sneakers, long dark hair, dark blue backpack, with his arm in a make-shift sling, the other 5'10", black hoodie, jeans, and backpack with red sneakers. He carried a big, bright yellow kayak paddle.

I waited until they boarded the boat, then returned home, and called the police station to arrange a reception party at the other end.

"My work here is done," I said to myself as I sipped my coffee and made my way to the front porch. My friends would be up soon, and I couldn't wait to hear their versions of the harrowing adventure of the "Kayak Rustlers."

I was also anxious to learn how things went in town, so I called the police station.

I wish I could tell you the two suspects were apprehended, pleaded guilty and made restitution, the islanders patted me on the back for my fast thinking, and the police commended me for my powers of deduction.

However, that is not what happened.

"No, ma'am," the desk sergeant said. "The shift has changed and the island liaison has the day off. Would you like to leave a message? I can put you through to his voice mail."

It's true, the long arm of the law didn't reach the island on this occasion.

All suspects remain at large.

DEVIL IS IN THE DETAILS

As the Constable, I was on duty 24/7. It was a position of honor, not of financial reward. I was paid $17.21 a week and my retirement fund accumulated at $.02 a month. My primary duty according to the Council was to act as police liaison for my community; my primary duty according to my community was to keep the Police as far away from the island as possible. My boss, the island liaison from the Police Department, had little to say. He understood, as I was to learn, there was really little to nothing effective the police could offer in the way of help. In order to respond to a call on the island, they would need two free police officers, four free firemen and one free fire boat to get them all here, by which time any self-respecting criminal would be long gone.

The first year of the job was relatively quiet, even when the summer folks arrived and the population increased to +/- 300 on a weekend. I believed few islanders knew there was a new constable, and those that did, called about noise – barking dogs, loud music or lawn mowers revving up before 7am.

The parameters of the job changed dramatically when the Island Liaison called me in June 2002:

"Fran, you know that new private development on the end of your island? Well, even though they have their own security, they are entitled to City police protection too."

"What does that have to do with me?" I asked.

"Your beat just doubled, Fran."

"Lt., it also more than tripled the population and potential problems. The majority of these folks will show up by 4th of July and leave the second week in August. Summers will be crazy. Do I get a raise?"

He was still laughing as he hung up.

The following day as I walked with George, he said, "Oh, it will change all right, Fran. Just you watch. If it's going to happen, it will happen in August. Neighbors are tired of neighbors, kids don't want to go back to school and the tax bills arrive."

George's words were accurate. The initial calls concerning barking dogs now included fights over parking spaces and missing bicycles. My observation skills from art school served me well as did my meditation practice: I arrived on scene calm, cool, collected and with a keen eye for detail.

If possible, complaints were resolved on the spot. If need be, I invited folks back to my front porch to discuss the matter while I disappeared into my kitchen to prepare some refreshments. By the time I returned, the involved parties were likely to have reached a solution of their own making. However, not everything could be solved so idyllically.

DEEP POCKETS

Summer was in full swing on the Island. Kids rode bicycles everywhere: to adventures in the woods, to the sandy beach, to either or both ends of the island to jump off the docks, to the pool, to the bowling alley and then to the General Store, a.k.a, the 'candy' store.

The 'candy' store was located in an old restored brick building, a stone's throw from the dock, the perfect location for kids seeking sweets.

Penny candy was a thing of the past although the names were the same: Kit Kat, Skittles, Heath Bar, Hershey Bar, Ring pop, Almond Joy, Tootsie Rolls, Rolos, Mike and Ike, Juicy Fruit, Hubba Bubba, Sweet Tarts, and gold foil wrapped coins in a mesh bag. Kids loved them and Ron, the proprietor of the General Store, loved the kids.

One sunny afternoon I received a phone call from Ron.

"Is the Constable available, please? This is Ron at the General Store."

"Yes, she is, Ron. How can I help you?"

"I have three young men with me who I just caught stealing candy. I would like you to come down to interrogate them."

"Are these younger than 12 yr. old men, Ron?"

"As a matter of fact, that's correct."

"Do you know their parents?"

"No, I do not."

"See if you can get some names and a phone number and I'll be right down."

I put my camera, badge and notebook in my bicycle basket and rode down the hill to the General Store.

Ron was sitting outside at a table on the porch under a bright blue umbrella. Three young boys sat with him.

"Good afternoon, Ron. Boys, I'm the Constable and my name is Ms. McNulty. Do you know why I was called here?"

The older boy, perhaps 11, said, "He says we were taking candy." Ron replied, "I know you were taking candy because I saw you put it in your pocket and leave the store without paying."

"OK, let's get your parents down here to sort this out. Do any of you have cell phones?"

All three took a phone out of their shirt pockets.

"Where are you staying?"

"Up at the parade ground," the oldest boy said, glaring at me the entire time.

"Do you know the address of your unit?'

"No."

"Each of you please call your parents and when you reach them, hand me the phone. I'll speak to them."

The 11 years old said with a smirk, "No one's answering."

Ron shook his head sadly. He said, "I'll be inside if you need me. I gotta get back to work."

The 9-year-old said, "No one is answering my phone either," but the 8-year-old boy said, "Are we going to jail?"

"Well, that will depend on Ron, I suppose. But most likely not." And with that he handed me his phone.

"Hey Robbie, what's up, buddy?"

"Hi, my name is Fran McNulty and I'm the Constable here on the Island. Are you Robbie's father? …I have Robbie with me at the candy Store. He's fine but would you please come down here, we have an issue over shop lifting…Yes, two other boys are here also…No, this is not a joke. I would appreciate it if you come as soon as possible…Oh? Well, my choices are to call the Police or talk with you first…Yes, we will be right here."

Robbie's dad showed up on a bicycle moments later. "What's going on?" he asked as he bounded up the steps to the porch.

"As I said on the phone, all three boys were seen stealing candy from the store by the owner. I would like to ask the boys some questions and have them empty their pockets in your presence so we can determine what went on."

"That sounds reasonable."

"For the record, can each of you give me your names?" I asked as I took up my notepad.

"Robbie Gunther," the youngest said. "They're my cousins."

"I'm Stevie Gunther," said the middle boy.

"Joseph T. Gunther, Jr.," was the oldest one's reply.

"Robbie, did you take candy from the store without paying for it?"

"Yes, we all did," Robbie said with big sad eyes.

"Stevie, did you take candy from the store without paying for it?"

"Yeah," he said as his brother kicked him under the table.

"Joseph, how about you? Did you take candy from the store without paying for it?"

"You can't prove anything."

"Ron," I called, "would you come out here for a moment to witness this?"

Ron wiped his hands on the apron that hung about his waist as he came out to the porch.

"Alright. Robbie, empty your pockets onto the table. And now you, Steve and Joseph, you can empty your pockets over to this side."

"Do as you're asked boys," Robbie's father said.

I stood in amazement as the boys reached into their cargo pants again and again and pulled out more and more candy. My camera clicked away.

"I knew it," Ron said. "I knew they were stealing me blind. There's got to be over $150.00 worth of candy there. And that's just today. I've been suspicious for days but really just caught them today."

"Boys, what did you do with the other candy you've taken?" I asked.

Between sobs, Robbie said, "It's under our beds at the house." Joseph T Gunther, Jr. rolled his eyes. Robbie's dad had trouble keeping his jaw closed.

"Well, let's walk up to your house now, while Ron inventories this pile. I'll hold your cell phones until we get there. Thank you."

When we arrived at their unit near the park, two women were stretched out in chaise lounges on the porch drinking what looked like margaritas.

"Excuse me, I'm the Constable, my name is Fran and I would like to know if these children belong to you folks."

"Yes, these two are mine and that skinny one belongs to my sister-in law there," one of the women said barely moving from the chaise.

"Hey guys, you're back early," a man said as he came out to the porch with a tray full of cheese and crackers. "And you brought a friend. Nice."

By this time, Robbie's father had parked his bicycle by the old wooden steps and joined us.

"We have a problem guys. Seems the boys have been stealing candy from the Store and some of the loot is supposed to be upstairs. Joe, you come with me while we take a look. Come on Robbie, you too."

Although not invited, I followed the men up to the second floor while Steve and Joseph sat with their mother who had yet to move. The kids' room was strewn with clothes, towels, toys and partially eaten pizza. Robbie's dad reached under each bed and pulled out a total of three large grocery shipping cartons, known locally as banana boxes. Just as Robbie had said, they were full of candy. Candy wrappers and empty candy boxes filled the space under the beds.

"Robbie, are there any other places you guys hid the candy?"

"No, Dad, we kept it all under the bed."

"Bring those downstairs then," I told the men.

"Well folks," I said when the three boxes of candy were on the picnic table alongside the cheese and crackers. "I'm going to have Ron come pick these up and total the damages before he decides what he wants to do about this. Given the amounts, this may not be minor shop lifting. The police may become involved. How much longer will you be staying on island?"

"We leave on Sat," Robbie's dad said.

"OK, I'm going to seal these boxes and get Ron up here. I'll get some contact information from you as well. We'll be in touch."

"Joe, just write this Ron character a check and be done with it," Mrs. Joseph T. Gunther said.

Joe, Sr. reached for his wallet.

"If that's what Ron decides, you'll need cash or a credit card. He doesn't accept checks. Now if I can get your particulars, I'll be done here." By the time I had written down all their contact information, Ron had retrieved the merchandise. I returned the three cell phones and headed down to the Store.

"What a haul," I said to a smiling Ron as he parked his golf cart piled with the three boxes of candy. He had an even bigger grin as he prepared to break the duct tape seal and document the contents of the boxes. "I believe you can charge up to five times the value of a stolen item for compensation and with the price of your candy, you'll be able to retire."

"Offered me $500 on the spot. And I was tempted but I gotta tally this up first. I couldn't figure out how they were getting away with it, then I realized it was the cargo pants with those deep pockets."

I left Ron under the blue umbrella with his grid sheet and his calculator. I headed home to a cocktail of my own and to reflect on what nabbing an 8, 9 and 11-year-old did for my professional reputation.

PAULTON PERPS

Between deep sobs and long gasps for air, the woman was difficult to understand over the phone.

"Ma'am, please slow down. I'm having trouble learning why you've called. Can you tell me again what's happened?"

"A gang… attacking…sob…gasp… house. A gang… from Paulton. They're going to kill us."

"Ma'am, can you repeat your name for me and your address?"

"My name is Marsha and I don't know the address."

I did a quick mental run through of all the Marsha's I knew on the island; and there was only one, a new arrival who lived down on the point.

I clarified the location with her, asked if she was in immediate danger and she told me the attack had stopped. I said, "I'll get help and be right down."

I logged in the time and date then called our city worker who lived on island, explained the situation, asked him to get his truck and grabbed my flashlight, radio, camera and headed out the door. Within moments Esty's dilapidated pickup stopped in front of my house and I hopped in.

"Esty, my son will be getting off the 9:30 P.M. boat just about now so let's see if we can grab him to help too."

Sure enough, as we rounded the bend near Plymouth St., Bill walked casually towards us.

"Hi, Mom," he said. "What's up?"

"Hop in. I need help with a call and I'm deputizing you."

"Uh-oh. A little action on the island tonight?"

"Allegedly a gang of guys from Paulton Island wearing black leather jackets are attacking the old Schyler house on the point. Folks there are very upset."

When we made the turn onto Water Street, I noticed a group of kids standing by the side of the road. I asked Esty to slow down. I recognized all of them, our local pack of teens and perhaps a few cousins all between the ages of twelve and fifteen.

"Hi, guys, what's going on?"

"Nothing. We were just playing flashlight tag."

"Any of you see anything different tonight down this way?"

"No, but some guy over there is yelling a lot."

"OK, stay put while we go see what's up."

All the lights in the old house were on but otherwise the scene was still. We could hear a woman crying as we approached the porch. I instructed Esty to walk the perimeter of the house, making note of what he saw. I knocked on the door and told my son to look and listen carefully. I wanted to get his general impressions of folks inside.

"Mr. and Mrs. Dalton, this is the Constable. I'm here because you called," I yelled when no one responded to my knocking.

Mr. Dalton poked his head around a corner from another room, ducked back and then came to open the door into the kitchen.

"You're who the Police Department sent out?" he asked as he dismissively eyed me up and down.

"Yes, and these are my deputies," I said as I stepped into the house and nodded to my helpers who were now behind me. Both of my men weighed in over 200 lbs. and stood over six foot. They made an impressive posse.

"Well, that's a little better. I want those guys arrested. They've been terrorizing my family." As if on cue, his wife and two children entered the room dressed in pajamas and bath robes, clearly all ready for bed.

"Mrs. Dalton, are you the person I spoke to on the phone?" She nodded yes and I asked, "Can you tell me again what made you call?"

"A pack of hoodlums from Paulton Island were threatening us," Mr. Dalton began.

"Mr. Dalton, I would like to hear from your wife first. Thank you. Mrs. Dalton?"

"Well, it was after dark and I had just gotten the kids ready for bed when I heard people talking outside on the lawn, so I looked out the upstairs window. No one should be on our property, so I called to my husband and told him someone was trespassing. Someone was in our yard. He went to the door and yelled. What did you say, dear? Oh, get the heck away from our house. I stayed upstairs with the children. When we still heard them, my husband told them he was calling the police. And so I did."

"Do you have anything to add to that Mr. Dalton?"

"Yes, those bastards were shining lights in the windows and I could see them running around the house next door. I had to yell several times to get them to leave."

"On the phone, you indicated they were from Paulton Island, Mrs. Dalton. What makes you say they were from there? Did you recognize someone?"

Again Mr. Dalton answered. "Paulton has a bad reputation. Hoodlums. I'm from Boston and I know a hoodlum when I see one.

"Would you describe one for me?"

"Didn't you hear me? I said it was dark. They had on hoodies and baggie jeans.

"Leather coats. They wore black leather coats."

"Can you remember what they said? What made you think they were going to kill you?"

"What else would they be doing on my property? I want them arrested. What are you going to do?'

"Mr. Dalton, my job is to let the police know what happened here and I can explain your options. You can fill out a formal complaint which will trigger a police follow up, or you can do nothing. Esty, did you see anything outside?"

"Nope, everything looks OK. No damage - broken windows or jimmied doors. A little trash by the side of the house but nothing else."

"It looks like whatever was going on and whoever was doing it have gone. Call again if you need to but it looks like the rest of the night will be quiet. Last ferry to town just left. I'll ask around to see what I can find out. I'll let you know what I learn."

As soon as we were in the pick-up, Esty said: "Something's fishy. Guy's been drinking and I can't imagine him yelling 'get the heck away from the house.'"

"He sure didn't think much of you, Mom."

"I know, so thanks for coming with me. You were great back-up."

"Well it's the most exciting thing I've done on this island," my son said.

Esty agreed. "Yeah, and the guy had all the lights on in the house. Made an easy target for these Paulton Island bad boys."

My son added "Hoodies and baggie jeans I might buy, even though it was dark. But black leather jackets? Nobody wears black leather jackets around here, do they? I don't think he knows what he's talking about even though he is from Boston. The wife seemed to be driving things, so maybe he's reacting to her hysteria."

"Well I'm thinking the lights he saw were flashlights and that makes me think of flashlight tag. Wonder just where our kids were playing? I'll ask around but for now let's head home."

Surprisingly the group of kids I spoke with earlier were still by the side of the road. As we rounded the bend, I asked Esty to stop the truck.

"Hi again. Got a few questions for you. You said you were playing flashlight tag, right?"

Only five heads nodded yes; the other four had vanished into the night.

"Now just where were you playing?"

"Over on the point."

"Get anywhere near the Dalton's place? They just bought the Schyler cottage and are here for their first weekend."

"Oh, we didn't know anyone was in that house."

"So you were playing over there."

One of the girls replied: "We may have run across their yard but we didn't know anyone was there. Honest."

I directed my next question to the young lady. "OK, so then what happened?"

She answered: "Well, the man came running out of the house and scared the dickens out of me. He cursed at us and told us …I can't say those words but he wasn't very nice and so we left."

"And you boys, what did you do?"

"Yeah, he's drunk and cursing like crazy. He threw a whiskey bottle at me."

"And…?"

The other girl piped in. "That's when Jake ran up and… and we all got out of there."

Jake poked her in the arm. "Shut up. It wasn't our fault. He's a jerk."

"OK, I'll tell you what's going to happen. I'm going home now and I suggest you do the same. You have until ten o'clock tomorrow morning to tell your folks what did happen here tonight because that's when I'm going to call each one of them to discuss this. Then I'm going to call Mr. Dalton and explain what I think happened. Now get."

When we got home, my son said he would see me in the morning. Then he added, "I'll keep my pants handy, just in case those Paulton perps return."

By ten o'clock the next morning I had heard from every parent but Jake's. Both girls' folks were making banana nut bread and chocolate chip cookies respectively to take over to the Dalton's as an apology and a welcome. One of the boys called and wanted to come talk to me so we set up a time when his parents could also be here. A few fathers were dropping off some beer for Mr. Dalton later in the day.

That left Jake. I called his house and his father said he couldn't talk then as he was expecting an important call. I said I'd be in touch later.

About one o'clock, the young lad who wanted to talk knocked on my door. His mother was with him and I invited them to sit in the rockers on the porch.

"Jimmie has something to say. Go ahead, Jimmie," his mother coached him.

"Miss McNulty, I'm sorry you had to come out last night but he was a real jerk. Mom, he was. He shouldn't have cursed at us like that, especially at the girls. We were just playing flashlight tag and he came running into the yard yelling and screaming like he was nuts."

"Be that as it may, Jimmie, you guys really scared Mr. Dalton and his family. He never heard of flashlight tag, so he didn't have a clue what was going on. And true, he didn't attempt to find out but neither did you kids explain anything or apparently stop. So, I'm going to suggest you go down with your Mom and apologize."

"No way. I don't ever want to see him again."

"I can accept that. Can you think of another way you can apologize?"

"We can write him a note or leave him a message," his mom said.

"See, your mom can help you with this and it wasn't intentional. It just got out of hand."

As Jimmie and his mom left the porch, he ran back up to me and whispered. "Jake really got mad and wouldn't let it go. But don't let him know I told you."

By two o'clock I had two phone calls from each of the girls telling me in strictest confidence that Jake had done some things he shouldn't have. It wasn't all innocent. He had banged on the doors and then thrown stuff at the house, shined the flashlights into the windows.

With this new information about Jake's role in last night's events, I banged on his front door after dark. Jake's father was unhappy to see me.

"I'm not used to being disturbed this late at night. What is it, 9:30?"

"Yes sir, it is. It was about this time last night I was called out as Constable for an incident involving your son. Has Jake talked to you about what happened?"

The father opened the door and ushered me into the sitting room. I took a seat.

"The kids were playing flashlight tag. He said some drunk was having a fit, yelling and throwing things."

"Well, it's now clear it was a little more than that, sir. Can Jake join us?"

"No, he's already in bed."

"Seems Jake retaliated and raised the ante by banging on the guy's door, which then escalated the situation into something it should never have been. Granted Mr. Dalton did nothing to help, but I have witnesses who collaborate Jake was instigating some pretty aggressive behavior. Mr. Dalton has the option to file charges and Jake has the option to apologize."

"Oh, is this some kind of intervention?"

"I call it accepting responsibility for one's behavior, especially when anger issues are involved. You would know better than I if it's intervention, sir."

I said good night and left the house but not before I heard Jake's dad yell:

"Jake, get your ass down here right now."

The following morning I called Mr. Dalton. He was less than excited with the information I gave him over the phone.

"What's the sense of filing a complaint? The Police should have sent out a swat team but instead I got Ellie Mae Clampett and two stooges. I don't believe a word of this flashlight game bullshit."

And with that, he hung up the phone.

My son went into town later in the day and reported seeing Mr. Dalton on the boat to the City. The Dalton's luggage took up three seats. Mr. Dalton was surrounded by an interested audience as he related his tale of danger and the less than glorious response from the local yokels.

My son's wife had all she could do to keep him from tossing Mr. Dalton overboard.

"It stinks, doesn't it," I said to my son when he got home. "Here I had tripled our usual police response, had eye witness accounts of what happened and a gang leader just about ready to confess but Dalton won't believe a word of it."

We both shook our heads and said in unison, "All suspects remain at large."

LAUGH OUT LOUD

There is only one road leading to the south dock; and it passes right by the house at the top of the hill, within 10 feet of the house at the top of the hill. Whether on foot or in a vehicle, passengers head down this hill by 6:45 each morning to board the first boat heading into town at 7:00 A.M.

My phone rang at 6:51 A.M. one Friday morning early in June.

"Do you know what time those idiots woke me up this morning?" a homeowner yelled into my ear.

"I know what time it is now, so is it safe to assume it was before this?" I asked. "And with whom am I speaking?"

"Don't be smart, Fran. I've listened to them all week. Going by the house, snickering, talking loud and laughing. All they do is laugh. They laugh so loud, they could wake the dead, not just me. There's a noise ordinance from 10 P.M. until 7:00 A.M; 7:00 A.M!"

"Beulah, are you talking about the people going down to the dock to catch the boat for work?"

"Why else would anyone get that boat every morning? They make excessive noise laughing and I want it stopped. You need to enforce the law."

"Is there a particular group that laughs or is it everyone that goes by on the road?"

"Oh, it's one certain person. You can hear his laugh a mile away."

"Do you know this person's name?"

"You know who I mean, Fran. He's the rude man with that red headed woman... Clarence something from the other side."

Oh Dear. I considered Clarence a friend.

"Ok Beulah. Are you willing to sign a complaint? I'll need an official complaint before I can act."

"Since when isn't my word good enough? I know the Police Chief and I'm calling him as soon as we are off the phone. I want this taken care of today."

"Well, I'll be here all morning so you can stop by to do the paperwork anytime before noon."

At 10:22 A.M., Lt. Milton, my contact with the Police Department, called.

"Fran, heard you have some laughing hyenas roaming around your island early in the mornings now. I'm thinking of sending an officer out with a dart gun, so they can be tranquilized and safely removed to a better location."

"Beulah or Clarence?"

"The law's on her side, Fran. 7A.M. is 7A.M."

"Funny how the bus that goes by at 6:05 doesn't wake her. Oh right, her bedroom is on the other side of the house. Lt., you and I both know there's been animosity between these two for some time now. I think she has it in for him."

"You mean since he called her a baby at some meeting?"

"Yes, I believe that was when it started but his exact words were 'don't be a baby'. We have more important things to do, right?"

"Oh yes, so do me a favor, talk to him."

I set my alarm for 6:15 the next morning, got dressed and went outside with my first cup of coffee. I heard Clarence before I saw him. I put on my bicycle helmet with the flashing blue miner's lamp and grabbed my ticket book. I stepped into the road with my hand up.

"This is official business. Are you Mr. Clarence Montaine?"

"Hey, Fran, you know who I am. What's up? What's going on?"

"I have a complaint here from Beulah and I'm authorized to issue you this ticket for laughing before 7 A.M. in the morning. No laughing, sir. I'll have to give you another ticket as it's only 6:45. Sir, that laughing has got to stop or it's another fine. Sir, can you hear me over all this laughing? Sir, Sir? You have to get up off the ground."

Once Clarence realized he needed to stop laughing or miss the boat, he promised me from now on he would tip toe past the house on the hill. I felt I had completed my duty, so I ripped up his ticket and sent him on his way.

Clarence was as good as his word. For the remainder of the summer, he could be seen not only tip toeing past the house in question but pirouetting, twirling and dancing his way silently down the hill early in the morning on his way to the ferry.

Boat passengers and awaiting commuters loudly applauded his daily routine.

THE LONG WAY ROUND

Malcolm was a dignified, good looking man, married and a year-round neighbor. He was well liked, a great cook and a complete gentleman. He and his wife, Sunny, often invited me to parties and while I would become friends with Sunny, Malcolm always remained aloof.

On one of our walks, Sunny began to cry and told me Malcolm had stage four lung cancer.

"He's only 52. We'll fight this with everything we have. We'll go to Boston, where ever. I'm waiting for Doc. K to call back. What will I ever do without Malcolm, Fran?"

Dr. Kueck, a fellow year-rounder and developer of a highly successful lung cancer procedure, did indeed call back and Malcolm was soon enrolled in experimental protocols, involving surgery and medications.

Islanders rallied around the couple; the men visited Malcolm weekly, walked with him while Sunny took a nap and later carried him in his wheelchair to parties or just out to the porch for sunshine. Women did their shopping, ran errands in town and listened while Sunny talked a mile a minute on daily walks.

Two years into their battle it was clear the fight was almost over. Malcolm could not sit for more than a short while; his appetite was failing and listening to his breathing was painful. Oxygen tanks followed him wherever he went like a sad dog on a leash.

Sunny continually told me she was making plans for a small wake when the time came. She would have Malcom's close friends, champagne and some snacks. There would be a few candles.

My phone rang at 7:02 P.M.

"Fran, Malcolm passed just moments ago. You better get over here," Malcolm's friend said. "I have to leave."

I knew an unattended death, one in which a physician was not present, had specific requirements from the Police. The body and scene must be sealed off until authorities investigated. I called in the situation and I headed across the street.

There was a small gathering on the front porch.

"You better get up there," Jim told me and nodded his head towards the top floor bedroom.

"It's too weird, she's losing it," Tess said, wiping her eyes and holding on to her husband as they walked away.

I entered the house and called softly.

"Sunny, it's Fran. I'm coming up."

"I am so sorry, Sunny," I said as I made my way up the dark narrow stairs, my hands on both walls as I managed the sharp bend in the old wooden staircase. An odd flicker of light caught my attention as I walked up the remaining five steps. I ducked my head beneath a low beam and entered the remodeled attic bedroom.

Malcolm was lying on the bed under a light blanket; staring at the ceiling. He was surrounded by votive candles, hundreds of lit votive candles on the bed, on the dressers, on the windowsills, on the chairs. Every flat surface was covered with blazing candles. Sunny was standing with a match in her hand gazing around the bedroom in a daze. Its flame was dangerously close to her fingers.

"Here Sunny, let me take that," I said as I blew out the match.

"Malcolm would like all the light. I think I need some more candles."

"Sunny, you've done a great job already. Come here and sit down."

I blew out the candles on the rocker, moved them to the floor and helped Sunny sit.

"Tell me what happened. Was the doctor here?"

"Oh, the visiting nurse was out at suppertime and told me it was just a matter of hours but she couldn't stay. He died about a half hour after she left. I just had time to get his friends here before he went. He just stopped breathing. He didn't even have time to close his eyes."

I was glad to hear what Sunny just said. The scene was already in shambles from a police standpoint but given a medical official had been on site so soon before this death, a full Police investigation would not be necessary. I called it in.

"He's still so handsome. Isn't he handsome, Fran?" Sunny asked.

It was true, he was still handsome but if I didn't get the candles off the bed, the entire house would go up in flames.

"Sunny, we are going to have to end this lovely vigil you've created. Malcolm is going to need to be moved, so I'm going to begin to extinguish the candles. Just wish him peace as I do. OK?"

Together we recited 'peace be with you' as each candle went dark. I turned on a small lamp.

"Wait, wait, he can't be moved yet. He'd die if he thought his friends would see him like this."

"What are you talking about Sunny? His friends were all just here," I said as I put out more candles.

"Yes, but they didn't know he had on Depends. We have to change him. You better close his eyes so he can't see us."

I could not follow her reasoning but his eyes needed to be closed while they still could be. I reached over the bed and lowered his lids.

Sunny grabbed a pair of Bermuda shorts from the dresser, whipped off the blanket, and began undoing the diaper.

"Grab his leg and pull that on him," she said as she flung the shorts at me. I grabbed them before they landed and did what I was told. I lifted each foot into the openings, surprised at how heavy his legs were.

"I'm going to need your help," I said but Sunny climbed onto the bed and lay down beside her half naked husband.

"No time for that now Sunny, I need you to help with these shorts," I said.

The phone rang and Sunny, interrupted from whatever she was thinking, got up from the bed.

"Yes, this is the new widow. Already? Yes, we'll have someone there. Thank you. Fran, that was the undertaker. They are getting ready to leave the City on the water taxi. We need to pick them up at the dock."

"OK. I'll call Traps. He'll go down for us. We have a half hour."

We finished getting shorts on Malcolm and sat down to wait.

"Is there anyone you want to call now, Sunny?" I asked.

"No, I've already called his mother and I spoke with his children after the nurse left. I'll call his first and second wife tomorrow. And like I told everyone before, we'll have a memorial here on the island after the burial. He was raised Catholic but that's only important to his mother so maybe there will be a mass or something."

We spoke intermittently for over an hour before the front door opened and Traps called up.

"Sunny, the men from DeMarco's are here. I'm sending them up."

Two men in dark suits and ties came up the narrow stairway, ducking their heads as they reached the landing and entered the bedroom.

"We're so sorry for your loss, ma'am. I'm John DeMarco and this is my son, Jess. Is this the deceased?"

"Yes, this is my Malcolm. Doesn't he look handsome?"

"Yes ma'am. We'll need to move him now. If you would like to wait downstairs…"

"Oh no. I'll stay right here, you might need my help."

"Sunny, let's stand over here so we are not in the way and if they need us, we'll be close by."

A sturdy black bag appeared out of nowhere and the two men quickly maneuvered Malcolm's stiffening body inside. Sunny looked away as they zippered it closed over her husband's face.

The younger DeMarco asked "Is there another way downstairs?"

"No", I replied, "there is just the one staircase."

The two men looked at each other, knowing they had only moments before rigor mortis completely set in. They lifted the body, swung Malcolm feet first off the bed and moved toward the top landing. The younger DeMarco stepped backwards down the stairs but it quickly became evident Malcolm was too long for this short, boxed in run of steps. They brought him back into the bedroom and turned him around. They tried again. This time the senior DeMarco was carrying Malcolm by the shoulders but soon found himself up against the middle landing wall. As he twisted to make the turn to the first floor, Malcolm's head began to drop and unable to control this shift in balance, the younger DeMarco raised his end and in that one simple movement Malcolm was wedged into the top segment of the stairwell.

"He's floating," the widow observed.

The two men never said a word but proceeded to stare at the stair case, each other and Malcolm. The only way to move the body now was to slide Malcolm's head over towards the steps downstairs while his feet moved up into the top corner. With a few grunts and strains from the funeral folks, Malcolm rubbed the wall one last time and stood on his head on the top step of the lower flight.

Head first, Malcolm made his way down to the living room, one step at a time.

Sunny and I waited a moment, then followed them downstairs. She sat on the living room couch, still staring off into space while the bottle of champagne sat uncorked in the ice bucket. Despite all her talking, reading and planning, nothing had prepared Sunny for Malcolm's death. I did not want to leave her alone; but perhaps in the quiet that filled the house after we left, she would sleep for the first time in weeks.

Outside, the plan was for the undertakers to ride to the dock along with Malcolm's body in the back of Trap's old pick up. Traps had even put down a tarp, but as we settled the body bag down, the aroma of old lobster traps and fish bait rose from the truck bed.

"Is there another vehicle we can ride in?" Jess DeMarco asked as his father covered his mouth.

"Yes," I answered, "Sunny's car is around back. I'll drive that."

Traps pulled onto the dirt road and took the first right hand turn.

"This isn't the way to the dock," the older DeMarco said.

"No," I answered. "Traps is going the long way."

A little funeral procession began as I followed behind the pickup; giving Malcolm a farewell trip around the island.

When we finally reached the dock where the water taxi waited, the receding tide exposed the mud flats glistening in the soft moonlight.

The DeMarcos stood open mouthed. Under the railings, the gangplank tilted at a 50% angle after a sharp right hand turn at the top. But Traps knew what to do and he organized everyone for the job ahead. He would lead the way, the younger Mr. DeMarco in the middle while the older Mr. DeMarco was assigned the top. Once everyone understood their placement, Malcolm was slid off the truck into waiting hands and they walked to the gangplank.

"One, two, three," Traps shouted as hand railings and the right turn approached.

In unison, the three men raised their arms skyward and hoisted Malcolm over their heads. They navigated the turn with military precision.

Malcolm left the island like a Viking warrior boarding his awaiting knarr for the long voyage home.

GOLF CART MAYHEM

Dirt roads, few cars, deer in back yards, bicycles everywhere, no traffic lights or street signs all encourage the feeling the Island is safe and secure. So much so, folks leave their keys in whatever means of transportation they are using. Get off the boat and need a pickup truck? Well, you just borrow the red one sitting there with the keys in it as long as it's back where you found it before the next boat arrives. The same is even truer for golf carts, the preferred mode of transportation, as one key fits all.

The phone rang at 7:10 A.M. on a mid-August morn. I was not quite ready to begin my day so I got my note pad ready and let the call go to the answering machine.

"Fran, I can't find my golf cart. I'm sure it's been stolen. Can you give me a call at 7201?"

I poured my coffee, yawned and sat down in my rocker.

The phone rang at 7:30 A.M. "My golf cart is missing. Give me a call when you get this. It's Jonesy."

I sipped my coffee and moved my rocking chair a few inches into the sunlight.

The phone rang at 7:33 A.M.

"Fran, I know you're there, pick up. Fran? Oh hell, I can't find my friggin' golf cart. Call me. Oh, it's Rich."

I stretched my arms overhead, and wondered if there was a full moon last night.

My first call was to 7201, a new homeowner, Mrs. Joy Scobie.

"Mrs. Scobie, this is Fran. Tell me about your golf cart?"

"It's not where I left it. Someone has taken it."

"When did you last use it?"

"Last night. I came up from the restaurant and parked it by my porch and it's not there now. I looked all around the house but it's gone."

"Mrs. Scobie, is there anything distinguishing about your cart? Maybe a towel on the seat or decoration on the roof?"

"No. it's white and green and the rear seat folds somehow."

"Where are the keys?" I asked.

"Oh, they must be in my purse. Let me look…They're not there and I don't see them around. Did someone come into my house for them?"

"Do you think you might have left them in the ignition?"

"Oh dear, you are right. Yes… I left them in the cart. It seems so safe out here. I parked it right outside the house."

"It is safe, Mrs. Scobie. It's just that sometimes golf carts get borrowed and not returned properly. It hasn't left the island. I'll be on the look out for your cart and I'll give you a call later in the day."

I don't think she really understood, as she was anxious to fill out a report form.

My second call was to Mr. Jones.

"Morning Jonesy. I got your call and hope you had something specific in or on your golf cart that will help me identify it. When did you last have it?"

"It's not a good morning. What do you think the golf cart looks like? It's white and green and the rear seat folds up. I need it to pick up Sylvia on that ten o'clock boat. She'll be really pissed if I'm not there."

"I understand. When did you see it last?"

"Yesterday, after I went to the…no that's not right…I left it at the top of the hill thinking I would take a walk this morning and pick it up on my way to get Sylvia but then I decided to get my paper early. I walked all the way down there and the thing wasn't there. Then I had to walk all the way back here and I even forgot to get my paper I was so mad."

"I bet you're worn out, so why don't you think about who you can call to pick Sylvia up in case I haven't located your cart by then. We know it didn't get far and I'm headed out soon to take a ride around the island. I'll call you when I know more. Oh, one more thing. Do you have the keys?"

"You know I don't. I leave them in the ignition like everybody else."

My third call was to Rich.

"Hey, Rich, how's it going? I got your message about your golf cart. Any idea where you might have left it last night?"

"Fran, if I could remember that, I wouldn't be talking to you now, would I?"

"Suppose you're right Rich, so let me ask you this. No offense but what's the last thing you do remember?"

"Mm mm…I was down at the restaurant…ordered something to eat…couple of drinks, the usual. Two guys from town came in and we were talking about their 2005 Nautique super air 210. Oh yeah, then Floozie Susie came in. I hadn't seen her in forever so I had to talk to her. Did some dancing too. Bought her a few drinks before they closed."

"That's good Rich. Did you offer Susie a ride home?"

"Maybe. It's all fuzzy."

"Tell you what Rich, I'm heading out for a spin around the island so I'll keep my eyes open. You still have that 'ooga, ooga' horn on the front?"

"Yeah, but the cart is green and white and the back seat flips up for storage."

"Right."

I got dressed and headed down to the dock on my bicycle. I noticed something was going on at the Hinks place. Every possible water toy you could imagine was out on the front lawn. I waved as I went by and a teenage boy looked at me like I was crazy. Bet they are renting, I thought.

As I crested the hill, I saw Old Millie by her garden fence, so I stopped to say hello. She was always up on the latest news as her kitchen window faced the road and she saw everything as she slowly washed her dishes.

"Hi Millie. How are things around this neck of the woods today?"

"Well, I'm fine but Jonesy isn't. I could tell by the way he was walking, something's got his goat. Bet his wife is coming back. And Hinks got a bunch of wild renters at his place. Kids were up hooting and hollering till late."

"Anything specific or just the usual?"

"Well, since you ask, I think they got their hands on a golf cart which I know Hinks doesn't have and wouldn't include in the rent if he did…"

"MMM…I just might go introduce myself to them in a bit. Can I bring you your paper, Millie?"

She nodded no, so I said my goodbyes and rode down the hill. When I got to the dock, Esty was untying some knots in his lobster lines.

"Morning Fran," he said. "All quiet on the home front?"

"A flurry of calls this morning. Nothing major. Three golf carts had adventures last night and I'm trying to locate them. See anything?"

"Well, I did see two teens riding around after dark in one. Didn't recognize them but one had on a red and black plaid shirt. Not many kids around now with school starting soon. Think Timmy's here with his cousin but the college kids are already back in class, the rest of them are getting hair cuts and new clothes. Yep, summer is almost over."

"I know. My favorite season is coming up." I sighed in anticipation of the peace and beauty that descends on the island as summer folks close up cottages and we year-rounders transition into our fall rhythms. Then I grabbed

my paper, tucked it into my bicycle basket, waved to Esty
and pedaled up the hill.

Given what I now knew, I decided I would stop and
say hello to the renters. The young man I waved to earlier
was shaking a rug over the porch railing. I pulled onto the
lawn, lowered the kickstand on my bike and walked over
to him.

"Morning, I'm Fran McNulty and I live just down the
road in the red house with yellow trim. What's your
name?"

"It's Tom."

"You folks renting or are you relatives?"

"Oh, we're renting. We got in last night and will be
here for a week. It's great." He began folding the rug and
as he did, I noticed a red and black plaid shirt on the
railing.

"The reason I'm asking is I'm not only a neighbor but
also the Constable and we had an incident last night. Is
that your shirt?"

"Er...... yeah."

"OK, Tom, I've a couple of questions for you. Think
you could get one of your parents to join us.?"

"Uh, well I suppose so."

In a matter of moments, the boy and his mother
came out of the house.

"Ma'am, my name is Fran and I'm the Constable here
on the island. Last night a golf cart was taken from the
top of the hill up from the dock. Two boys were seen
riding around in a cart and one was wearing a red and
black plaid shirt similar to the one on the railing. I'm
wondering if Tom might tell us what he knows about it."

"Tom, did you and Joey steal a golf cart when you were out last night?"

"Er, um… er… We only took it for a little ride and the keys were in it so we didn't really steal it, Mom."

"That's no excuse. Geeze, we just got here."

"Tom, where did you leave the cart?"

"Um, we put it in the woods on the path."

Tom's mother cuffed him on the back of the head.

"And the keys?" I asked.

"Oh. They're in it."

"OK, let me go call the owner. You might want to get some shoes on Tom, Ma'am, cause we are going to retrieve the cart in a moment."

Mr. Jones picked up on the second ring. "Jonesy, it's Fran. I've located your golf cart and we'll be bringing it down to you in 'bout ten minutes. Will that work for you?"

"I thought you were Sylvia, telling me you were staying longer. But this is good news. Yeah, bring it down here. Who had it?"

"Apparently a kid whose family is renting for a week. What would you like to do about it?"

"As long as I get it back before that damn boat comes in, we don't need to do anything."

"OK, we'll see you soon."

I found the golf cart exactly where Tom said it was and I didn't see any obvious dents or scrapes on the cart. He and his mother arrived.

"Mr. Jones has indicated he won't press any complaints so I'm suggesting you and your Mom work out a nice apology while you follow me over to his cottage. The police won't be involved this time but I can't promise that if it happens again."

I pulled off the dirt road as we approached Jonesy's place. Tom's mother stopped behind me.

"I'll wait here while you return Mr. Jones' property, Tom. It's up to you if your Mom goes with you."

"No, I think I better do this myself."

We watched Tom knock on the door, we watched Mr. Jones come out onto his porch, we could see Jonesy gesturing wildly but we couldn't hear a thing. As Tom quickly walked back towards us, I waved to Jonesy and he waved back. I got on my bicycle and headed home.

One down, two to go.

I stopped at my home for some water before I made the trip around the upper section of the island which included an old army fort. I rode over to the restaurant keeping watch for out of place golf carts. Everything looked fine by the waterfront and the sun beamed off the water as it rose over Oyster Island to the east. I turned around and huffed my way back up the hill. It was still early for residents here and the old parade ground was very quiet. As I approached the deserted pool area, I spied a green and white golf cart parked in a flower bed. The ooga ooga horn on the front was bent to one side of the tree trunk.

I rode over to Rich's unit to give him the news. He was sitting out on his second floor porch. He was wearing a chartreuse robe and it looked like his hair was waving to me. I waved back, pointed to the pool area and he gave me a thumbs-up. Two down, one to go. I continued my ride.

As I rounded a corner, I encountered the shuttle van for the Resort beginning its daily run and pulled over to speak to the driver who also had some security duties there.

"Morning Jim," I said. "What a beautiful day. Things quieting down for you on this side of the gate?"

"Beginning to. Yeah... some. Last night we got a couple of calls. Still a few renters around, so noise is an issue. But there was one call about guys driving crazy in a golf cart. Somebody big and somebody with red hair. Haven't figured that one out yet."

"Well, Joy Scobie is missing her cart this morning. You have any kids fitting that description?"

"No, all the teens have gone home. We only have screaming babies."

"Lucky you. Well, I'm going to continue my ride. If you hear anything, give me a call."

"Will do. See you later."

Mm mm... a big guy and one with red hair driving crazy. Sounded like kids to me. Since the only other kids on island beside the renters were Timmy and his cousin, I decided to ride to the lower road where he lived. At 15, 6ft 3, and 200 lbs., Timmy easily fit the description of a big guy.

I knocked on the kitchen door and Timmy's mother answered. She had a cup of coffee in her hand and her husband was right behind her.

"Morning guys. Is Timmy around? Looks like some kids went joy riding in a golf cart last night and I would like to see if Timmy knows anything."

"Why are you always picking on Timmy?" his step dad bellowed.

"Didn't mean to come across that way, but I'm hoping he can tell me who was on island. Seems a kid with red hair was with a big guy driving crazy and I don't know anybody with red hair. Hoping Timmy can help."

"Red hair?" his parents said together and went back into the house.

I could hear the two of them yelling for Timmy and someone named Steve to get downstairs.

When the boys appeared, it was clear they had just gotten out of bed. Timmy's dark mane was flat as a pancake while Steve's red hair was sticking up all over the place.

"Morning boys. I'm here because a golf cart is missing from down at the resort and the owner is very upset. There was a report of a big guy and a guy with red hair driving erratically last night and was wondering what you might know about that."

"If you stole that golf cart, I'll kill you, you scum bag," Timmy's step dad said.

Immediately Timmy's mother stepped between them and almost took the punch her husband threw at the boy.

"Let's take a moment here folks. This isn't a major crime. The owner just wants her cart back. Let's take a seat and give the boys a second to reflect on what they can tell us."

Steve spoke first. "We were late so we thought if we used the golf cart we wouldn't get in trouble but then Timmy realized we couldn't get through the gate with it, so we went to the beach to come around that way…"

Timmy continued "but we got stuck in the sand. We were gonna take it back this morning. We just borrowed it."

"OK. Can you get some shoes on and show me where the thing is? I'll get Resort Security to help tow it out, depending on the tide and then we'll see what the owner wants to do. We probably can avoid police involvement if atonement can be worked out."

"What's atonement?" Timmy asked.

"It's part of saying you're sorry. You do something for the worry or damage you caused; like offering to wash the thing every week for a month or mow her lawn. Something like that; you work it out with the owner."

"Oh," both boys replied. They went to get dressed.

Timmy's step dad got up from the chair.

"Some sissy way to treat this, Constable. He should get a good whack to his head," he said, as he flexed his substantial muscles, made a fist and gritted his teeth.

"Look, no one wants the police involved either for the golf cart or for assault. You realized you almost hit your wife when you went for the boy before? Let's get the golf cart back where it belongs and go from there."

"Ah, you're right but no need to call that security guy, we can get it out ourselves," Timmy's step dad said as the boys came back downstairs.

"We can give that a try," I replied. "Lead on," I said to the boys.

The golf cart's front wheels were buried in soft sand just above the high tide mark.

"We're going to need a rope and a tow to get that out. I'll get security."

"Hold on. No need for that," the step father said.

And before I could reply, Father, son and cousin simply picked the golf cart up and had it on firm ground within minutes.

Timmy's mother quickly told her husband to go back to the house and forcefully added "I'll help them return the cart and make sure they come back home."

"I see you've found my golf cart. Is it all right?" Joy Scobie said as we pulled up to her porch.

"Seems to be but I suggest you take it for a spin to make sure. We'll wait here."

While we waited, I asked the boys what they were going to say. It was clear Tim's Mom had helped them with a response.

"You're right, runs just fine. So, what happens now?" Mrs. Scobie asked as she pulled up.

"We can file a complaint if that's what you want but I hope you will hear Timmy and Steve out. I'm going to finish my ride and will stop by on my way back. Whatever you decide is fine with me, Joy."

As I turned the corner on my way back, I saw Joy standing outside supervising the boys as they scrubbed her golf cart.

"Everything settled?" I asked as I pulled up.

"Yes, I'm satisfied," Joy said. "Thanks."

Three for three. I headed home to have my lunch.

THE CRAPPER CAPER

There is something funny about port-a-potties. Whether it's the garish colors, the outrageous company names like Royal Flush and Blow Brothers or just scatological humor at play, people find them funny. And if you can move one on someone...that's a real kicker.

One day a port-a-potty was shipped to our island intended for a construction site about half mile from the dock. For a variety of unimportant reasons, the contractors who arranged for this delivery did not arrive the same day as the port-a-potty and so it was left on the dock: spanking clean, wrapped in shrink wrap and in everyone's way. There it sat for a week.

Some folks ignored it, some folks muttered about it and some folks complained out loud. None complained louder than the owners of a lovely hill top home, just up the road from the dock. They sent emails stating how their view was contaminated, how our collective reputation down the bay for law and order was now a joke and how the island was being spoiled by transient residents. They went on to name one person as the main source for our slide into disgrace.

Facts have little to do with opinions and as I was to learn, these folks were not even on island when they spread their opinions about 'abandoned' cargo and island behaviors. To make matters worse, almost our entire population is made up of transient residents - we call them summer people - while the targeted suspect lived here year-round and voted on island for the last fifteen years. So just about everyone – winter and summer people - were upset by these electronic outbursts.

As the island Constable, I don't go looking for trouble, try to stay out of harm's way, avoid gossip and live a quiet peaceful life. I do not read my newspaper until after lunch nor do I turn on my computer over weekends. So, I was unaware of the energy being put into stirring the port a-potty.

My first hint of trouble was a phone call from the mainland police. They called me on a bright Sunday morning about 11:00 A.M. They had just received a complaint from an out-of-state home owner who said someone had put a, you guessed it, port-a-potty on the front porch of her island home. I was needed to go investigate immediately. The police officer I spoke with had trouble talking without laughing as he assigned a case number with the label the 'Crapper Caper'. The urgency of the call baffled me as I was sure the port-a-potty wasn't going anywhere.

I gathered my incident report forms and my camera; put them in the basket on my bicycle; donned my helmet and pedaled to the scene of the crime. I try not to prejudge a call until I have some facts but one question popped into my mind - how did folks so far away know about this?

The view of the bay is beautiful from the top of the hill. You can easily see 180 degrees and it is said on very clear days, you can see all the way to Spain. I approached from the rear of the house, parked my bike near the side door and walked around to the front porch. Sure enough, a bright blue green port-a-potty was sitting smack square in front of the door like underwear on the clothes line for the whole world to see.

I snapped several pictures for the record and noticed a tour boat pulling close to the shore line. Are they off course? I wondered. No, they were just getting in better position so passengers could also get good pictures of island living. I waved and they waved back.

I looked around for signs of damage to the steps and the port-a-potty. No signs of forced entry. I checked for tire tracks on the lawn but there was no evidence a truck or any other vehicle had driven across the yard. How had they moved that thing? I wondered. Pretty impressive and definitely not a one-man job.

I called in my report and was asked if I could find out who the equipment belonged to. Then I was instructed to get it out of there one way or the other. Apparently, the home owner was threatening to call the mayor and the pressure was on. Not enough pressure for the police to come out and investigate themselves, but pressure nonetheless.

My first call was to the freight shed at the ferry line and the second to the contractor who had paid the freight bill. I explained the situation and the urgency of a solution but somehow failed to instill the appropriate response in the contractor.

Besides he couldn't get out to the island for a few days. I suggested he call a friend on island who might be able to pitch in and move it because if it was left to me, I would tie a rope to it and pull it with my bicycle. He finally agreed to call in a favor.

Later that evening, I walked by the site and saw a pickup truck on the lawn in front of the porch. The tail gate was down, level with and overlapping the decking. I watched two people 'walk' the structure from the porch onto the truck in four easy movements. They waved and I returned the greeting.

"Hey Fran, if they wanted a second bathroom, they should have called me," the driver yelled.

Criminals 1, Constable 0

ALIEN INVASION

The regular Sunday night gatherings at this home or that were enlivened by the retelling of the first time folks spied the now famous 'port-a-potty on the porch' incident; but no one hinted who the perpetrators were, if anyone knew. The island quieted down.

Not so the homeowners who were still away. They called the city Police at least twice a week asking for, then demanding, updates on the old investigation. The police naturally called me. I would relate I had nothing new to report and that was that, until August.

August was, as my friend George told me, a time when things happened. Everyone was in a bad mood.

Sure enough, on Aug 2, at 8:15 A.M., my phone rang. This call from the Police department was very different from those earlier in the summer.

"You have a hate crime on your island and we are sending a uniformed officer out to investigate."

"A hate crime?" I asked. "What happened?"

"We've just had a call from a homeowner who is out of state reporting someone has written hate messages on their lawn. We need you to do a preliminary investigation."

"And what's the address?" I asked.

"Says here, it's at the top of the hill up from the dock."

"Oh, dear," I said.

"Yep. Our guy will be out on the ten o'clock boat."

As I gathered up my camera, bike helmet and report sheets, the phone rang again.

"Fran, we've had it. I'm at my wits end. My good jewelry is in that house and I need to know if it's still there. It's in an old coffee can in the freezer. The spare key is under the side porch on the left. Someone is targeting us; they've probably been in my house. I feel so violated. You are supposed to protect us and you've done nothing all summer to keep our property safe. Go down right now and look, then call me back immediately."

"I'm going down now to meet the officer who'll be doing the investigation. I'll wait until he gets here before I go in your house... Yes, I understand you're anxious. I'll ask him to call you when we're done."

I hung up and hurried out of the house before the phone could ring again.

I did my deep breathing exercises to help me focus on the task at hand - riding my bicycle safely down to the house in question and meeting the boat from town. I did wonder what time it was out where the homeowners were.

I met Officer Graves as he got off the boat and introduced myself. We took a moment to look up at the house from the dockside angle. The lawn looked newly mowed. Nothing caught our attention and we walked the 100 yards to the front porch. We tried all the doors. Each was securely locked and all the windows were intact.

Officer Graves located the key and we went inside. The interior was neat and clean and the family jewels were still in their hiding place.

"This all looks OK. Let's check upstairs," the officer said.

"That will give us a better view of the lawn," I said.

We looked out the second story front windows, the side windows and the rear windows. We peered, squinted, turned sideways and almost upside down but we saw nothing unusual in the grass below that even hinted at a message.

We came back downstairs and walked the tracks the lawn mower had made, we took samples of the soil, we looked for paint spray, gypsum, oil and gas. Nothing.

"Well, what do you think?" Officer Graves asked me.

"I think it was done at night in special ink that disappeared as the sun came up. So, perhaps it was seen by a late flight in or out of the jet port."

"I'm thinking UFO's myself," he said.

"Can I get a copy of your report?" I asked him as he boarded the ferry back to town. Then added: "Oh, and don't forget to call the homeowner."

He didn't wave as the boat pulled away.

There was a message for me to call the homeowner when I got to my house. I decided to wait for the party to call back and made a list of questions I might ask if the investigation were mine:

How did the homeowner learn of these hate messages?

Did they know the names of the informers?

Did the informers say what time they noticed these messages?

I also wondered what these folks were on. Not very non-judgmental of me I must admit.

The homeowners never called me back, I never received a copy of Officer Graves's report and yes, all suspects remain at large.

THE BIG STINK

The fluorescent blue green of the Blow Brothers port-a-potty twinkled among the darker shades of the yew trees near the barge landing. I noticed it as I walked by on one of my strolls around the island.

The port-a-potty sat there for three days awaiting the right high tide for transport off-island, not an unusual sight in and of itself for construction sites anywhere in rural Maine. And not an unusual sight on the island because the one barge company servicing the Bay was heavily scheduled and had limited operating hours when you factored in the weather, man hours and the tides themselves.

The barge landing with the port-a-potty was situated across the street from a very expensive waterfront home in an exclusive gated community and caused the homeowner considerable aggravation. He began to notice a distinct smell.

On the fourth day, he decided he had had enough. He started up his back hoe, gingerly grabbed the port-a-potty, carried it across island and relocated it outside the residence of the Homeowner Association's president. "See how you like looking at this," he said to no one in particular as he drove away.

As it happened, the president lived in one of seventeen 2-unit condos on a circular drive surrounding a green expanse of lawn. Many residents were treated to the exciting colors and aromas of the structure and emails with pictures were sent to those who were off island for the event.

Later that same day, the irate property owner attended an unrelated meeting between the city fathers and island residents from both sides of the gates. During a lull in comments, this homeowner stood and complained about the unsightliness of piles of trash placed near the road at most everyone's home in anticipation of our annual heavy item trash pick-up. "The island looks like a dump" he told the crowd, most of whom lived outside the gates of his community.

I myself enjoyed the green grassroots recycling efforts of heavy item trash pick-up. I've found some nice old rockers for my front porch and a lovely brass lamp amongst the piles.

While the City meeting was taking place at one end of the island, the Homeowners' Association president down at the gated community called their property manager to take care of the offending port-a-potty. He in turn, acted quickly, relocating it to an isolated area where it again sat twinkling among the yew trees awaiting tides favorable for transportation.

Point made; problem solved.

Apparently not everyone agreed. Under the cover of darkness, a few unnamed persons rounded up every broken, discarded toilet they could find in the heavy item pick up piles. They also grabbed all the baby furniture they could find in the trash piles and delivered it all to the lawn of the waterfront property. Why the baby furniture? Perhaps it suggested the owner was acting like a child but that is only my guess. If they were seen, those who witnessed the act never broke the code of silence.

My phone rang just before 9 A.M. the following morning.

"My property has been vandalized," I was told. I said I would come down to take a look. I put my report forms in the basket that was tied on the back fender of my bike with a bungee cord, got on and stuck the blue LL Bean head light on my helmet. I pedaled over to the scene. Some say the head lamp is pretentious but I found it added comic relief to delicate situations and tensions often subsided as I approached.

But not that day. The property owner was livid. His pristine lawn was covered with commodes, play pens, potty chairs, car seats and cribs of all sizes and colors; twinkling among the grass and yew trees like gems on green velvet. As far as I could tell, there was no physical damage to his house, his belongings or his yard. He had the property manager take photographs before the day laborers began the clean-up process. Clearly, I had not been his first phone call and yet his face was still bright red. A vein on his forehead throbbed with each word of outrage he yelled at me.

"I want you to catch these people from the other side. They didn't like what I had to say yesterday. It's your job, so do it."

I explained my role as Constable, I explained the complaint process and I explained his options.

"We don't know for sure it was the folks from the other side," I said. "Perhaps this is a reaction to your moving the port-a-potty yesterday and is the work of your immediate neighbors."

"No, it's those people on the other side of the gate. They didn't like me telling them they lived in a dump and I demand justice."

We filled out forms and I pedaled home to file the report.

Two hours later, my phone rang again. Someone had blocked the lower road and gate with a back hoe, effectively restricting access between the two sides of the island. "Yes, I will come down to investigate," I said but not before I called the police station for guidance. My instructions were:

"Get it moved, it's a safety issue."

I pedaled down to the lower road and saw a group of neighbors standing around looking at the back hoe. No one was shy about sharing what they had seen. I pedaled over to the waterfront property I had visited just hours before.

The house looked spectacular, not a blade of grass out of place. I found the home owner in a heated debate with the property manager in front of the house, totally ignoring a breathtaking view across the water. Their conversation stopped as I approached. I stepped right into the silence.

"Sir, you were seen leaving your back hoe in the middle of the lower road. Can you tell me what happened?"

"I'm protecting my property from those vandals on the other side."

"I see," I said. "However, it's a safety issue, sir. The fire truck and the ambulance need to get through in case of an emergency. The back hoe needs to be moved as soon as possible. Can you do that for me now, sir?"

I believe if the property manager hadn't felt the need to repeat every word I just said in a voice loud enough to be heard over on Oyster Island, the afternoon might have gone differently. However, he insisted upon screaming 'it's a SAFETY issue', 'it's a SAFETY issue', until I finally asked him to leave the area. As he walked away he said:

"I'm calling an emergency meeting of the Board of Directors to address all these infractions. Then you'll be sorry."

The homeowner yelled at him as he walked away. "You're a f....ing idiot."

Once the property manager was out of ear shot, I said "Be that as it may, it's time to move the machine," and the homeowner went to get the key. I followed behind the back hoe as he drove it to a storage shed and I thanked the owner for his cooperation. I pedaled back home to complete my paperwork and called in the all clear to the Police.

I was just stirring from my afternoon nap, when the phone rang yet again. This time it was the property manager.

"He tried to kill me. I've got witnesses. You gotta get over here. I want to sign a complaint."

I grabbed my forms, got on my bicycle and headed over to his office. I found him sitting at his desk. He looked terrible.

The story unfolded as he wrote out his statement. The Board of Directors had met to discuss the moving port-a-potty and the back-hoe incident. They had invited the property manager and the homeowner to present their sides of the issues. At some point, the homeowner allegedly leapt from his chair, grabbed the manager by the throat and attempted to strangle him. The red finger marks and early bruising gave proof to his words. I took notes from the remainder of his remarks, the names of witnesses, photographed his neck and advised him to see a doctor. I asked him if he felt safe and he replied he was leaving the island for a few days.

I pedaled back home and called my report in. The desk sergeant was astounded by my busy day and instructed me it was not over yet. I needed to get statements from each of the witnesses at that meeting. I made the necessary phone calls and headed out for the first interview. Four of the six people present when the violence occurred now refused to answer my questions. The two who did cooperate corroborated the manager's account.

Again I made my way home. I felt incredibly tired and deeply saddened by how we treated each other. I wondered how it would all be resolved.

As a result of all the meetings, the Board of Directors ordered the construction site crew to get the port-a-potty off island immediately. The crew moved the port-a-potty down to the barge landing early the next morning but they missed the tide by half an hour. It sat awaiting transport for another three days while the smell intensified and the fluorescent blue green color twinkled among the yew trees.

The property manager sued the homeowner and they settled out of court.

All other culprits remain at large.

FENTON

I see myself as an Officer of the Peace and am of the mind we should solve our own problems when possible using common sense and island logic. For the most part, it worked well. However, there was one situation when I didn't know how things would work out.

His name was Fenton and while he certainly seemed human at times, he was a dog, a big black dog. He sniffed crotches, played fetch and ran free. Fenton was lucky because he had owners who thought dogs should be able to sniff crotches, play fetch and run free. The City, however, thought dogs on the islands should come when called or be on a leash. Since our dog population was increasing along with golf carts and homeowners, summer was full of nice dogs barking greetings to everyone they met.

Fenton was a nice dog, not a good dog. Good dogs came when they were called, never got into the garbage, never peed on peoples' feet, always pooped in the woods and never, never chased other dogs when they were riding in golf carts with their owners. Good dogs always waited patiently for you to greet them, walked by their owner's side, obeyed commands, and never begged. Come to think of it, Fenton never begged. He simply took whatever food caught his sense of smell from wherever it happened to be: in a child's hand, on your front porch grill, in your LL Bean bag or on a table when a romantic dinner was under way. Fenton was not shy. It was just a matter of time before Fenton ran afoul of the law.

As it happened, Fenton loved a sweet yellow lab named Cana. She was a good dog and flattered by the attention Fenton showed her. Try as her owners might, they could not keep Fenton away. I believe their efforts simply increased his ardor.

One afternoon Cana was napping at home while her owners were off island. It's my guess Fenton passed by the ground floor apartment where Cana lived. He caught her scent and knew he had to be with her. He gently nudged the front door expecting it to open because no one locked their doors on the island but it would not give.

Stronger measures would be required. He slammed into it, waking Cana who began to entice him with her sexy barks. He put his shoulder to the task and this time he crashed through the hand tooled wooden screen door to be with his love. He went on to entertain her by ripping up every pillow and cushion on the couch. They were just heading into the kitchen for a bite to eat when Cana's owners came home.

My phone rang moments later.

"You have to come arrest Fenton. He broke into our home and destroyed our furniture."

I grabbed my rope and camera, got on my bicycle and headed over to Cana's house. Oh boy, Fenton, you've done it this time, I thought. When I arrived, the owners were on the front porch shaking their heads as they looked at the damaged screen door. I saw Cana sitting in a corner but Fenton was nowhere to be seen.

"Can you tell me what happened?" I asked "and where is the dog you're complaining about?"

"He's that big black one, Fenton. You know him. We had him cornered when we got home. Look at the mess he made."

"My new cushions are ruined," the woman cried.

"We almost had him but he slipped between the two of us and ran out the hole in the door."

With the information I had, I took a wild guess and headed down to Fenton's house; and clearly waking the owners from a nap, I asked if he was at home.

"Oh, yes," his owners said. "Take a look."

Fenton was sitting on a rocker on the back porch and actually yawned when he spotted me. His owners swore he was out there the whole time. He looked very comfortable and I would have been inclined to agree with them except for two things: the white feathers stuck to his muzzle and the piece of screening around his neck.

I cited Fenton on suspicion of Entering and Destruction and set up a hearing on my front porch for an hour later.

All parties arrived as expected including both dogs. I gave my instructions: come to some terms you can both live with or I call Portland and we press formal charges. I told them to call me when they were finished and I went inside.

About a half hour later there was a knock on my door. Cana's owners told me they decided if the screen door was repaired and the sofa cushions replaced, they would be happy. Fenton's owners agreed. I set a time frame for the work to be finished and figured my job was done when the two couples told me there was one more agreement. Cana and Fenton would have supervised play times in the hopes of producing an offspring.

I swear Fenton smiled.

CHANGING TIDE

To my mind nothing indicated the changing nature of our island more than the following story. Our population was slow to recognize the community was becoming a suburb rather than a rural outpost. The Island Liaison told folks at a meeting, "The next five years will see the island 'grow up' as opposed to being a rebellious, unruly teenager." The writing was on the wall.

As Constable, I had many encounters with a dog named Alphonse and his owners about his behavior. Neighbors, visitors, and officials called me to complain and off I'd go to find him, put a rope on his collar and take him to my house. I tied Alphonse to my tree, gave him some water and called his owner to come get him. When she arrived, she rolled her eyes, sighed and shook her head, then took him home.

One late summer day, I was called because Alphonse was pestering a group of folks trying to fish off the pier. He liked to fish and could not understand why the children wouldn't share the bait. So he was helping himself. He came with me willingly and I called his house only to learn his owner was away for the day but his grandmother was in charge. I brought the dog to her and told grandma to keep him tied.

I walked into my house while the phone was ringing; Alphonse was now going through someone's garbage and spewing it all over the road. I captured Alphonse and again told grandma to keep the dog tied. This time she didn't even wait until I was off their property before she opened the door and let him out.

When I returned Alphonse the third time, I told grandma she was going to get a ticket if she didn't keep the dog tied. He could not run loose and yes, I understood Alphonse was upset because his owner was away.

And so it was quiet for several hours. I went for my customary walk and was almost home when suddenly, Alphonse ran into me, caught me behind the knees and almost brought me down. I managed to maintain my balance and grabbed his collar. Again I tied Alphonse, gave him water and called his house and this time, the owner answered.

"Oh, just let him go, he'll come home," she said.

"I can't do that because this is the fourth time today he's been here. You have to come get him."

I did not feel I needed to wait on her to get the dog, so I went about getting ready to meet friends. I had just showered, was wrapped in towels head to foot on my way to my bedroom when I heard a tremendous banging at the front door. I stuck my head around the corner and was seen.

"You get out here, you coward. I have some things I want to say to you."

"Look, come in and have a seat. I'm just going to get dressed."

"No. You get out here now."

I moved to the doorway and opened the door as to let her in but that never happened. She began a tirade accusing me of everything from ruining the island to being a pervert. Her voice ran loud and clear and every other word was interrupted with a swear word or two or three.

As it happened, a woman was walking by and naturally stopped to listen. I could see her but the dog's owner had her back to the road, so she could not.

I knew enough not to engage this woman or verbally defend myself but when she said

"If I had my gun, I would go home and shoot these f...ing dogs and you better watch out."

I knew I needed to end this.

"That's it. It's time for you to go now. I want you off my porch. This is over." I watched over her shoulder as the silent observer moved behind the tree line.

The dog's owner glared at me with more hatred than I have ever seen, grabbed her dog and stormed off.

A head popped out of the bushes. "Are you all right? What was that about?"

"It was all about the dog. I'm OK but boy, am I glad you witnessed what was happening. Thanks for sticking around."

But I was not OK. I felt sick to my stomach. My entire space had been contaminated by her anger, spite and venom. It clung to me like tar and I wanted to take another shower to cleanse myself of her filth. But first I needed to call into the police station and report what had happened in case she followed through with her threat.

The first thing the officer I spoke to asked was did I feel safe, did I need backup? Those were nice questions but in reality, here on the island backup is at least 20 minutes away. And when I thought about it, I did not feel she would come after me. She had a reputation for these 'blow-ups' but as far as I knew, once it was over, it was over.

I wrote up my report, took another shower and went on to meet friends for dinner.

Two days later there was a message on my answering machine.

"If you watch yourself and stay out of my way, I suppose you can still come to my party."

Perhaps this was her way of apologizing but I had never heard of such a thing and felt no one would believe me if I related what she said, so I asked the earlier witness to come listen while I hand wrote the message for the police. I had no intention of going to her party now and my absence most likely gave Alphonse's owner permission to tell everyone how horrible I was. I heard later most folks thought being constable had gone to my head and I should have let the dog go.

I could live with not going to the party and not having support from fellow islanders but I definitely wanted a pay raise or at least a parking place in town for my efforts in the name of the City Police Department. "Good luck with that," the desk sergeant said.

I was surprised a week later when the Dog Warden called me. He had never called before. He was coming out to the island on Wednesday to give Alphonse's owner a ticket for letting her dog run. I was to meet him at the

2:45 ferry and escort him to the address involved. I was also instructed not to inform anyone of his arrival.

I have to tell you Alphonse is not the only dog to go unleashed on the island. However, the other dogs do come when called and seldom do the kind of damage Alphonse has been responsible for. So I knew the Dog Warden was likely to encounter a few dogs on our walk to Alphonse's home unless folks knew to keep them either tied or indoors. I decided not to tell anyone he was coming in an effort to be fair. Deep down I felt if I had gotten a little more support around the first incident, I might have decided differently. Besides once folks see a police man on the ferry, word spreads down the bay like wildfire alerting anyone who needs to be alerted. The die was cast.

On the afternoon in question, I went to the ferry at the appointed time and had to smile when the big black lab arrived there too. As the Dog Warden stepped onto the dock, the dog jumped on him in greeting and the Lt. asked whose dog it was. No one there acknowledged poor Alphonse. I stepped forward, introduced myself and the dog. The Dog Warden looked around for a slip of rope, found what he wanted and quickly leashed Alphonse for the walk home. I could see cell phones coming out of pockets as we headed up the boardwalk - the island was now on full alert.

When we arrived at Alphonse's home, I was told to knock on the door, ask for the owner and when she came, ask her to get some identification then wait down on the grass.

"That means do not move and do not say anything." With that, the dog warden stepped to the door.

"Is this your dog?" he asked. When she answered yes, his next question was "Can I see some identification?" She immediately went into outraged mode; no stopping at curious, upset, or indignant. Her voice bellowed across the water towards the City.

"What the fuck? Is she responsible for this? You're a policeman, get her off my property."

"I need to see some ID," he said in reply.

She slammed the door and disappeared from view. She returned with her wallet and her mother. Now Grand mom began to yell as she pointed at me.

"She's done nothing but bother me all day. Arrest her for harassment."

"Madam, will you please go back inside?" the policeman asked Grand mom. "And you ma'am, why don't we come down off the porch?"

Grand mom complied but opened the kitchen window and continued to yell "She's ruined the island. Get her off our property."

Meanwhile, the dog owner glared at me as the policeman asked to see the dog's license.

"He doesn't have one," she answered, "And if it weren't for her, Alphonse wouldn't need one."

The warden proceeded to tell her that was not true and he was issuing her a ticket for not having her dog licensed.

The woman went into overdrive outrage and tore up the ticket. The policeman told her he was giving her a ticket for letting the dog run loose. The woman went into raging overdrive outrage and began to point her finger at him.

"Ma'am, you need to calm down. This is a minor infraction but if you don't calm down, things will get worse."

"It's all her fault," she yelled as she pointed at me again. "She is a bitch and she's had it in for me since my son peed on her shoes."

"Ma'am, you need to calm down. This is about the dog not being licensed and running loose, clear violations of the City's animal control laws."

At this point, her husband sped into the yard in his pickup truck, jumped out of the cab and rushed up to me. He effectively placed himself between the Dog Warden and me.

"You're responsible for all this. You called the cops on my wife. No one calls the cops on my wife."

Lt. Palmer was alert to it all. "Sir, stand over to the left, please, and show me some ID if you would."

"What the fuck is this? Everyone knows who I am."

"Sir, this is about the dog not being licensed, so if you are part owner of this dog, I would suggest you show me ID or stand away from this area where I can see you."

"Honey, it's your dog, so I think I'll go stand right here." He was still too close for my comfort.

"You like having me close to you, don't you? You, bitch, you," he said in his sweetest voice.

The dog warden addressed the woman again. "Now ma'am, here are the two tickets…" She took them out of his hand and ripped them up, yelling even louder that she would see me in the hospital.

Grand mom, who was still leaning out the window, called "I'll get the gun, Horace."

Horace yelled, "There are no guns in the house, Ma. No guns in the house."

At this point, the warden said something to the dog's owner very quietly and she shut her mouth immediately. She told her mother to close the window. The officer turned and walked towards me, the husband scooted to his wife and they went inside.

"Just walk calmly off the property towards the road, don't look back." I did as I was told.

"You did great," he said. "I don't think she likes you very much. Just so you know, she received a ticket for harassment and was slapped with a restraining order in addition to the two other tickets."

"I was so scared. I can't help thinking about what could have happened."

"Do you feel safe out here by yourself?"

Good question. But the answer was yes, I did feel safe. I did not believe she, her husband or her mother would do me physical harm. They might tell lies and try to intimidate me, let the air out of my tires but not physically hurt me. The dog warden walked me to my home and filled out his report.

"Call me if they bother you, OK?" he said and then he walked away.

Word spread around the island faster than a forty mile per hour wind but I did not talk about the incident to anyone.

It was inevitable I would meet these folks at the ferry dock and within a week they were boarding the same boat into town as I was. It's impossible to stay 50ft away from anything at the dock but I did not expect them to get immediately behind me as we boarded. I was hit in the shoulder with a backpack as the husband shifted the packages he was carrying. Once onboard, I sat down as soon as I could, next to a friend from Oyster Island and they passed by.

As I rose to leave the boat I was aware of someone crowding me from behind. I turned and there was the man, glaring at me, his wife behind him.

"What's that horrible smell?" the wife asked in a very loud voice.

"It's right around here," the husband replied "and it's rotten to the core."

"You think they wouldn't let anything that smelt that bad on the boat. You guys smell that back there?" she asked the line behind her.

"Phew, it's worse than bad bait," he said.

"Yeah, should be thrown overboard."

They laughed hysterically.

I did not look at them or respond to their taunts in any way but I did stop to call Lt. Palmer. I needed support and I wanted him to know what they were up to. The desk Lt. who answered the phone wanted to know the nature of the call. I gave him a brief summary and then he said,

"I'm sorry, ma'am, Lt. Palmer died yesterday of a heart attack. Did you want to talk to someone else?"

"No," I replied. My hand was shaking as I pressed the off button on my phone. Breathe, I told myself, breathe.

THE GOLF CART WARS

The dictionary defines trespassing as 'going beyond the limits of what is considered a legal or moral right'. When I first arrived on the island, trespassing was defined by those who happened to be around. Since the winter population was 17 in the early days of my residency, there was never an issue, even though some of those 17 folks lived in the gated community to the north. Most people off island till summer were grateful that friendly eyes were checking up on things: foot prints in the snow around a window, blown-open doors, or house damage from a storm.

Within two years of my arrival, things began to change. A population explosion meant a chicken in every pot or a buggy in every portico and before you could say 'dinner's ready', the south side of the island was overrun with 50 golf carts. Finding a spot at our eight-bay parking area in time to make a ferry was impossible. Gone were the days when people walked or called the island taxi for a lift. Liability issues, no-shows, and the driver who cursed like a drunken sailor, all led to the demise of the service. Things were also changing in the north side development, a.k.a. the Resort. Old military barracks turned into condos were selling like cigarettes at the commissary. Each property sold came complete with a thick red book for development policies and a thick blue one for Homeowners' regulations. Concerned citizens on both sides of the gate as well as interested uptown institutions and out of town organizations (Audubon,

Island Institute, DEP) referenced particular sections, paragraphs and page numbers to ensure their rights were protected.

> The right to peace and quiet
> The right to the way life should be
> The right to complain and make trouble
> The right of old growth forests
> The right to make money

While I was Constable, the gates had been opened, locked, reopened, and closed but unlocked. This issue heated up with the weather and as the summer population arrived, folks were either ecstatic with all the new faces and places to visit or appalled for the same reasons.

There was a summer south side organization, the north side community's Homeowners' Assn. and the year-round group comprised of folks from both sides, the Civic Assn. It was hard to keep it straight. Despite all the paperwork in the policy books, one rule caused the biggest problem: article 72, Section 7.4, page 167, paragraph II - "No traffic shall pass from the north side of the island to the south".

The rule was clear enough but no one really paid any attention to it since traffic meant vehicles, including golf carts, the primary means of transportation on the island. And if the gates were open, the possibility of now over 200 golf carts fighting over eight parking spots did not bode well. Clearly something needed to be done about traffic.

The City was happy to let residents work it out in a democratic manner. They also knew, as long as we were fighting amongst ourselves, they didn't need to do a thing. My immediate boss, Capt. Milton, instructed me to follow the city's lead. The north side Homeowners' Association was content to lock the gates during a long five-month summer season while some members of the South side were adamant all rules be enforced all the time as long as those rules didn't apply to their particular circumstance. The Civic Association sided with the North but viewed summer as a two-month season. Months of deliberation and acrimony followed.

One day a rumor spread over the island like fog from the sea. It went something like this.

"They almost have it. I heard the Island Talks are reaching a good compromise," Esty told me as we waited for the inbound ferry.

People waiting on the dock perked up their ears.

"Well, what is it?" I asked.

"Eight and four…open from Nov. until May. Closed then until Oct."

"Makes most sense to me, although May can get crowded down here as folks open up cottages."

"Everyone will have to be considerate for May, Fran. Park at the top of the hill, share rides, that kind of thing."

"Ha, ha, ha. It'll never happen" one man, everyone called Snake, replied. I had never seen his forked tongue but I watched his beady eyes gleam with malice as he spoke.

The ferry docked and everyone boarded. Snake made his way out to the fan tail on the lower deck. He looked over his shoulder and then quickly pulled out his cell phone.

"I just heard they're going eight and four...Well, when will they vote?" ...Everybody the same day? Oh, I get it....Everyone coming? I'll see you at Harley's tonight then."

He closed his phone, looked around again and put it back in his hip pocket.

Later that evening, six members of the north side Homeowners' Association were having wine at the President's condo.

"Glad you all could make it,' he said to the small group gathered around his dining room table.

"I've looked over your latest email, Chester, and I think we can live with this," the Vice President said.

"I agree. I'm only out here in the summer, so I don't care if the gates are open the rest of the year," added the Secretary.

"It gives us winter folks a little more flexibility around that sparse boat schedule. Don't have to run the shuttle back and forth so much." Jim was a member of both the Civic Association and the Resort's Homeowners' group.

"Yes, would mean less gas and could mean we can get the van off island for maintenance," the Treasurer remarked.

"When do you meet with the other two groups?" the Vice president asked.

"Next week," the president said "and by then ballots will be ready for voting."

"More wine, anyone?"

At the same time, eleven members from a select group of families on the south side met Snake at Harley's house at the end of the Western Promenade. Almost all of those gathered were descendants of the original shareholders of the first Island development corporation of 1892. Inter-related thru marriage, ties ran deep. Children, grandchildren and great grandchildren had grown up during summers on the island when a caretaker looked after the board walks, wagons and farm produce. They did not keep change in their pockets or in their vocabularies.

"Glad you all could make it," Harley said. "By now you've heard the latest; there is an agreement which might be acceptable to most everyone."

"This 8/4 plan is a passable business and we need to be ready to vote within a week," said O'Neill, the south side's representative at the Island talks.

"So how do you want to proceed?" Harley asked.

"Proceed, I don't want to proceed. Can't we delay again?" asked the Boston businessman.

"Delaying isn't going to change anything at this point," said O'Neill.

"What do we have for votes?" Mrs. Small, Harley's sister, asked as she looked over the membership list.

"If ballots were to go out with proxies, we could control more than half of them but we can't insist on proxy voting at this point," added O'Neill.

"Why not?" asked one of the lawyers.

"Neither of the other groups vote that way – they're talking a simple yes or no response. Look, I've sat in on all the meetings and that piece isn't going to fly. We missed it in the beginning. Who ever thought it would get this far, anyway?" O'Neill lowered his eyes then busied himself with papers.

"We didn't miss it, you did," said his cousin.

"It is what it is – what can we do about it?" remarked the retired diplomat.

"Well, I've an idea," said the Bostonian. "We can threaten to sue the city if they don't lock the gates per the original agreement. The City will cave. They don't want any lawsuits."

"Oh, I like that." said the lawyer. "It will stop the voting process cold and won't cost a bundle."

"It's all in the timing, ladies and gentlemen, all in the timing. Here's what we need to do."

They worked late into the wee hours and when they finally said good night, the developer had a draft of a document he would take to his lawyer in the morning. He even had two fat checks in his wallet to go along with it.

It wasn't until the following day the year-round Civic Association gathered at Andy's Old Port Pub before the 5:45 P.M. ferry home.

"Good job, Traps," Esty said to the wizened old lobsterman who headed this group. "I think everyone can live with 8/4."

"Well, everyone at the table gave something and got their most important point, so it's really a good compromise. Even O'Neill agreed in the end. Now the vote will be a formality and then it goes before City Council."

"Raise your glasses to one island."

"Well, most of the time," Esty said.

"One Island" echoed through the bar and could be heard out on Commercial St.

Representatives of the three groups met the following Wednesday and drew up a simple ballot to be emailed to each property owner.

Traps was surprised how smoothly it all went. He had figured O'Neill would raise the proxy issue one more time and briefly wondered if he should be worried when O'Neill didn't. He dropped the thought as the representatives from the three organizations shook hands.

On Friday morning, Ms. Patricia Rogan, the lawyer for the City, called the City Manager as soon as she opened the envelope from Jim Kelly, Esq. The formal Notice of Filing to Sue was on his desk within minutes and he immediately placed a call out to the gated community.

"As President of the Homeowners' Association, Chester, I am informing you the gates between the north and south side of the Island must be locked immediately."

"What the hell happened?" Chester asked.

"We have changed our position and are adhering to the original terms of your development."

"What the hell happened?" Chester asked.

"That's all you need to know. Lock those gates."

Chester heard the line go dead and hung up his receiver.

"What the hell happened?" he asked his empty dining room.

News spread like an allergic reaction.

"The City is locking the gates."

"O'Neill threw us under the bus."

"Here's to a quiet, peaceful summer at last."

The other copy of the pending law suit made its way into my post office box and was waiting for me that very morning when I took the ferry into town to retrieve my mail.   Other than the twelve families who signed the document, the City Manager and the City lawyer, few people knew I was named co-defendant in the pending law suit. The charge was 'dereliction of duty for failing to uphold the laws of the City and the terms of the original ordinances'.

Something deep inside me burst and I knew my time as Constable was over.

Lt. Milton anticipated my resignation and called to meet for lunch. Despite his compliments for a job well done, he could not convince me to reconsider. I handed him my type-written letter effective immediately. The position of Constable has remained vacant since 2004.

Neighbors complain about neighbors, dogs run amok, outhouses get moved and golf carts get borrowed. Shouts of "One Island" can be heard late at night after a party or two and there is still a parking problem at the ferry dock during the summer. We live in a lawless society and I wouldn't have it any other way.

AN ISLAND'S JOURNEY

Not quite a mile square, mostly ledge and clay, cooled by breezes from the bay in summer that then howl in winter, the island was first inhabited by livestock and Indians before an 1892 land deal changed its face and its name. New investors mapped out ¼ acre lots on their third of the island, cut down all the trees, established an Association and put up a for sale sign.

They laid out roads, named them but never got around to putting up street signs; the rural character appealed to new owners. House numbers were assigned according to construction and summer homes built by well-known architects still stand. Forward looking owners purchased four lots and built in the middle of them to ensure elegance and breathing room. Cottages were full in the summer, closed down for the winter. Some names of original owners still grace the tax rolls.

The roads were called Crystal Ave., Moon Rise Lane and Sunset Blvd. The summer colony flourished until the 1970s when the economy shifted, women entered the work force and the first year-round residents showed up. They referred to the streets as the Lower, Upper and Middle Roads even though the Middle road was the highest of them all and the Upper road was in the middle of the island. Mosquito Alley, Princess Point, Clam Flats, Walter's Park, the Ball Field and Store Beach were and still are well known locations not indicated on any map.

Deepwater anchorage and an ice-free bay attracted the government and they built a military fort on the second third of the island in time for the Spanish American War, then abandoned it after World War II. Pieces and parts from the now-empty base made their way into just about every residence on the bay; and if someone yelled "Attention", most of the houses would need to stand and salute. In the 1980's the first attempt to reuse/restore the fort as a resort was made only to collapse in bankruptcy. A second effort with new investors failed. The third try was a success - a gated community without a fence.

The last 90 acres on the island were privately owned and remain so today. It is a large tract of woods and streams, ponds and cliffs, gullies and gorgeous views. It abuts my back-property line.

Acknowledgements

My thanks to members of the Casco Bay Writers' Project. (John, Steven, John, Mary, Beda, Susan, James, Dr. John, Tom and Linda) and the Gang of Six (Val, Sue, Tom, Mariam and Jane)

Additional thanks to all the colorful island residents whom I encountered during my years as Constable and who continue to make island living such an adventure. A special thanks to the Police Force for their understanding of island affairs.

A thank you for the legal advice I received from Chris Leddy, Esq., Bethann Poliquin, Esq. and the Maine Writers and Publishers Association. Pat Graham, John Ford.

Weberanne3@gmail.com